A Bed Full of Cats

Holly Keller

Green Light Readers
Harcourt, Inc.

Orlando   Austin   New York   San Diego   London

Flora is Lee's cat. She is as soft as silk. Flora sleeps on Lee's bed. Lee likes it that way.

When Lee moves his feet under the quilt, Flora jumps on them. *Thump!* When Lee wiggles his fingers under the sheet, Flora tries to catch them. *Swish!*

When Lee pets her, Flora purrs.
Purrrrrrrr...
When Lee sleeps, Flora sleeps, too.

One night, Lee had a bad dream. He wanted Flora. She wasn't on his quilt.

He moved his feet, but Flora didn't jump
on them. He wiggled his fingers, but Flora
didn't try to catch them.
He wanted to hear her purr, but Flora
was not there.

The next day, Flora was not in Lee's room.
She was not on Lee's bed.
Lee didn't know where Flora was.

"You should try to look for her," said Mama.
"We'll help you," Papa said.
"She'll come home when she needs to eat,"
said Grandma.

Lee looked for Flora in the house.

Mama looked all around the garden.

Papa looked in the trash bins.

Grandma looked up in the peach trees.

Flora didn't come home. Lee was very sad.
His eyes were full of tears. If only Flora
would come back! "Please come home,"
Lee cried.

"We could put an ad in the newspaper," Papa said. "What should we write?"
"Write this," said Lee. " 'We lost our cat, Flora. If you find her, please call.' Then give our number."

Lee didn't hear anything about Flora. No one found Flora, and she didn't come home. Days and weeks went by.

Then one night, Lee felt something on his
bed. He moved his feet under the quilt.
Thump! Thump, thump, thump, thump!

He wiggled his fingers under the sheet.
Swish! Swish, swish, swish, swish!
Lee sat up and turned on his lamp.

"Flora is home!" Lee yelled. "And that's not all!"
Mama, Papa, and Grandma all ran to see.
There was Flora—with four kittens!

Now Lee has a bed full of cats, and he likes it that way. Those cats are as soft as silk. They are also fun. *Thump, thump. Swish, swish. Purrrrrr!*

Think About It

1 Where did you think Flora was as you read the story?

2 What would you have done if you were Lee and your pet was gone?

3 What did the author do to make the end of the story a surprise?

A Book Full of Pets

In the story, Lee loves his cat.
What are your favorite pets?

WHAT YOU'LL NEED

- paper
- crayons or markers
- tape
- pencil
- stapler

Think about one of your favorite pets.

Draw a picture of the animal on a piece of paper.

Write the things you like about the animal on another piece of paper. Tell why you would like to have that kind of pet.

When you are done, tape the two pieces of paper together.

I like fish.
They swim.
They are pretty
to watch.

I love dogs.
They play with you and
they are good friends.
My dog licks my
face all the time.

⭐ Think of other pets you like. Draw pictures and write about them, too.

🌙 When you are done, make a cover and staple all of the pages together. Now you have your own book full of pets!

My
BOOK
of Pets

Meet the Author-Illustrator

Holly Keller got some of her ideas for this story from the things that her children did. When her children, Corey and Jesse, were little, they wouldn't sleep without their favorite stuffed animals on their beds. Corey's favorite stuffed animal was a mother cat with kittens, just like Flora in the story.

Holly Keller believes that when you read, you find out about new places and meet all kinds of characters.

Holly Keller

For information about permission to reproduce selections from this book, write to trade.permissions@hmhco.com or to Permissions, Houghton Mifflin Harcourt Publishing Company, 3 Park Avenue, 19th Floor, New York, New York 10016.

www.hmhco.com

First Green Light Readers edition 1999
Green Light Readers is a trademark of Harcourt, Inc., registered in the United States of America and/or other jurisdictions.

The Library of Congress has cataloged an earlier edition as follows:
Keller, Holly.
A bed full of cats/Holly Keller.
p. cm.
"Green Light Readers."
Summary: Lee fears he has lost his pet cat Flora,
until Flora returns with a new family.
[1. Cats—Fiction. 2. Lost and found possessions—Fiction.] I Title. II. Series.
PZ7.K28132Bf 1999
[E]—dc21 98-55236
ISBN 978-0-15-204876-1
ISBN 978-0-15-204836-5 (pb)

SCP   15 14 13 12 11 10
4500703048

Ages 5–7
Grades: 1–2
Guided Reading Level: G–1
Reading Recovery Level: 15–16

Green Light Readers
For the reader who's ready to GO!

Five Tips to Help Your Child Become a Great Reader

1. Get involved. Reading aloud to and with your child is just as important as encouraging your child to read independently.

2. Be curious. Ask questions about what your child is reading.

3. Make reading fun. Allow your child to pick books on subjects that interest her or him.

4. Words are everywhere—not just in books. Practice reading signs, packages, and cereal boxes with your child.

5. Set a good example. Make sure your child sees YOU reading.

Why Green Light Readers Is the Best Series for Your New Reader

● Created exclusively for beginning readers by some of the biggest and brightest names in children's books

● Reinforces the reading skills your child is learning in school

● Encourages children to read—and finish—books by themselves

● Offers extra enrichment through fun, age-appropriate activities unique to each story

● Incorporates characteristics of the Reading Recovery program used by educators

● Developed with Harcourt School Publishers and credentialed educational consultants